In those far off dim and distant days before men fished with fishing rods and lines, the heron had short legs. He would go fishing in the shallows of rivers, streams, lakes, ponds and puddles and hope to catch fish. He fished by standing still on hot days, and by stalking on cold days; catching the fish with his spear-like bill.

Because he only had short legs
he could never go into the deep water and
so his diet was almost entirely made up
of tiddlers and tadpoles.

Although they were tasty, it took so many to fill him up, and it took so long to catch them, that he wished he could fish in the deep water where the big fish lived.

The brilliantly coloured kingfisher
also had a spear-like beak and he fished in
the deep water where the heron longed to fish.

But as the kingfisher was only small,
he lived on tiddlers too. He caught them by
perching over his favourite river or stream and
then diving on his dinner like a streamlined arrow.
In fact he only fished in the deep water
to avoid banging his head on the bottom
when he dived.

In those far off dim and distant days, ancient man copied the kingfisher. The fish in the shallows were too small and so the fishermen glided out into the deep water in canoes hollowed out of logs. They would stand, with spears and bows at the ready, to catch the great big extra tasty fish. They had to aim their spears carefully to make sure all the angles of the throw were exactly right – that is how fishermen came to be called anglers.

The heron looked on with envy – if only he could fish in the deep water like the kingfisher and the fisherman with his spear. Once or twice he tried to copy them – perching on an overhanging branch with his short little legs and diving towards an unsuspecting fish.

Unfortunately he always fell with all the grace
and speed of a fluttering feather duster. On one
occasion the wind caught his feathers and he
did a gigantic belly-flop; he disappeared
in a great cloud of spray and all the fish for
a mile upstream and a mile down-
stream dived deep, well away from
danger. Needless to say, the
heron caught no fish.

In those far off dim and distant days when the world was warmer, the heron looked on with envy at the pelican too. The pelican had webbed feet and a huge pouch under his bill. This meant that he could swim easily into the deep water, where he would dive. Then, when he saw a fish, he would scoop it up, using the pouch rather like a fishing net. Ancient man watched the pelican, as well as the kingfisher, and soon he was fishing with a net in addition to his spear.

In frustration, the short-legged heron tried to swim out to the deep water, like the pelican, but without webbed feet his legs simply splashed about and gradually his feathers became waterlogged. They were so heavy that to save himself from drowning he had to flap his wings, as well as kick his legs and make for the bank. It was the heron version of the breaststroke, and sometimes even the dog-paddle.

When ancient man saw this soggy spectacle, he did not want to copy the heron. He simply roared with laughter – deep, prehistoric laughter.

The heron who became the soggiest and wettest of all was Henry. Like all herons, Henry had another problem: not only did he have short legs, but his neck was as short as his legs. This meant that even if he caught a really big fish he could not eat it. When the fish's head was in his stomach, the tail was still wriggling about outside.

It was even worse with eels. Henry loved long slippery eels, but he simply could not eat them. His neck was so short that when the eel's head had been swallowed, its tail was still wrapping itself around his stumpy little neck, trying to stay outside.

If he persevered, and swallowed and swallowed, then, by the time the tail was in his stomach, the head was trying to get out elsewhere. This could be very embarrassing, particularly when having tea with friends. The eel would wriggle and squirm inside Henry and even tie itself in knots. Henry's stomach would bulge and bounce and he would burp, belch, and hiccup; he could not help it and felt most unwell. Because of this he gave up trying to eat eels.

Poor Henry had one other problem, even larger than the others. He was married to Henrietta and every spring they built their great stick nest on the banks of their favourite river, at about the time the frogs spawned. This meant that when their eggs hatched they could feed their family on thousands and thousands of tadpoles.

The trouble was, every year their eggs failed to hatch and there never were any baby herons. Each spring Henrietta laid between three and five beautiful light blue eggs and began to sit on them. Then, it rained; it rained and it rained. The water in the river got higher and higher and every year the precious eggs were washed away. Henry and Henrietta were always extremely upset.

One year they tried to make their nest watertight, so that it would not get flooded. They lined their nest with leaves and Henrietta laid her eggs; then it rained and rained and the water in the river rose higher and higher and the floods came, yet again. Soon the nest was floating away, with Henrietta still sitting on the eggs and Henry flying slowly behind. She floated for so long and so far on the current that Henry became tired; he had to perch on the rim of the nest to rest.

They floated on and on until they reached the sea. There, the tide and currents caught them. The waves got higher. The land got smaller and they felt very sick. The sea became rougher and rougher and the nest began to fall apart. Henry and Henrietta were in danger of becoming herrings, not herons and so they left their sinking nest to fly to land.

They were heart-broken
and as soon as the seagulls saw
the eggs unguarded, they swooped
down and ate them up.

Each year only a few herons in the entire world managed to hatch their soggy eggs into baby chicks and there was a risk that the heron would become extinct. Consequently Henry and Henrietta decided to have one more try. As they were building an even larger new nest by the river, in their usual place, the rooks were building their nests high up in their rookery at the top of some tall trees.

It was strange, because rooks' nests look like miniature herons' nests. Henry stopped work and thought. Roland the rook also stopped work and thought. He was a friendly, talkative rook and he flew down to see how Henry and Henrietta were getting on. "Why don't you copy us?", he said. "Build your nest in the trees – it looks as if you use the same design. The higher you go, the better the weather, and you get a wonderful view."

Henry and Henrietta looked at each other through their large yellow eyes. They thought and pondered, wished and wondered and then they decided. Their great spear-like beaks touched in a kiss, and they began to work. For five whole days, all day and every day, Henry and Henrietta dismantled their nest by the river and rebuilt it at the top of the tallest tree – a huge old elm. They flew up and down, down and up, all day and every day, building twig by twig, for five days, until the new nest was completely built – a nest with a view. Then, just as planned, Henrietta laid her three beautiful light blue eggs and began to sit on them straight away – to incubate them. She and Henry would have to take it in turns to sit, for 25 days and 25 nights, before the eggs would hatch into small, fluffy, heronlings.

Roland had been right. The weather did seem better up there, and even when it rained the water dripped from the nest and the eggs kept dry. If it rained and rained it did not matter, and the river in flood caused them no problems. Then, when the sun came out it seemed much warmer up there than down in the damp.

But Roland had forgotten to tell them one thing. Although the weather was better, the higher you build, the worse it becomes when the wind blows – for the branches at the top of the trees sway far more than those near the bottom. So when the wind blew, it reminded Henry and Henrietta of going to the fair.

One night the wind blew, and grew into a gale. It was the greatest gale that even Roland could remember.

Henrietta was swaying violently from side to side and was in danger of being catapulted out of her nest; without her on top of them, the eggs would quickly have been scrambled. She hung on with her feet. Henry was perching near her, gripping with all his might to the topmost branch of the tree, until his toes ached from the effort.

Henrietta found it harder. She wriggled her feet and made two holes in the floor of her nest; then she pushed down with all her might to hold on to the branch below with her toes. Like Henry, her toes ached, but it kept her safe and the eggs even safer.

The wind blew harder and harder; the tree swayed faster and faster and, believe it or not, as Henry and Henrietta held on, their legs began to stretch longer and longer. But it was not only their legs that grew, for each time they changed direction their heads wanted to keep going straight on, and so every time their legs were stretched longer and thinner, their necks grew longer and narrower too, until their legs and necks were almost as long as each other.

The sun came up; the wind died down, and Henry and Henrietta looked at each other and blinked. They were exactly how herons look today. They no longer appeared squat and comical, but with their long legs and elongated necks, they looked rather graceful and beautiful.

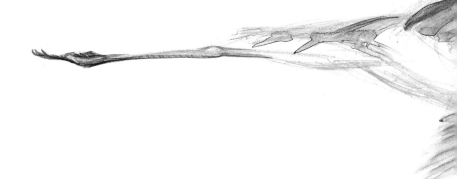

Henrietta felt hungry and Henry decided to fetch
her some breakfast. Suddenly, flying felt strange and
he tucked his neck in and trailed his long legs out
behind, in exactly the same way as herons tuck in
their necks and trail their legs today.

He landed in the shallows as usual. They were too shallow and his neck was too long to fish in comfort, and so he walked slowly into deeper water. The big fish were not used to seeing herons there, and soon Henry had caught a large snoozing carp and he swallowed it easily. It felt wonderful as it slithered down his long graceful neck – although its tail tickled him slightly.

Within a minute he had caught something else and he flew back excitedly to his broody wife, with his legs still trailing out behind. He gave her his very special gift – an eel, a long, slippery, slithery eel, the longest eel they had ever seen. She swallowed it without any discomfort or embarrassment and despite its wriggling it did not even make her hiccup.

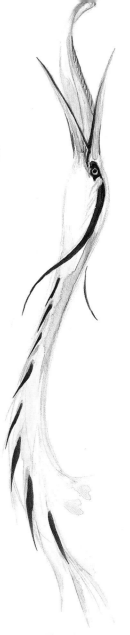

It was a happy spring. All three eggs hatched and the little herons, Izaak, Isabel and Iris, grew well. Izaak was the oldest, by one day, the first baby heron in history to have long legs and, like his father, he hung on by his toes in the wind. As soon as he could fly Henry took him down to the river to fish, and Izaak grew up to become the most famous fisherman there had ever been.

So, that is how the heron got long legs, and a long neck as well. Now the birds have to be most careful, for if their legs get any longer – how will they manage to sit down?

It was a happy spring. All three eggs hatched and the little herons, Izaak, Isabel and Iris, grew well. Izaak was the oldest, by one day, the first baby heron in history to have long legs and, like his father, he hung on by his toes in the wind. As soon as he could fly Henry took him down to the river to fish, and Izaak grew up to become the most famous fisherman there had ever been.